tkomovement.com

"Learn to read, change your mind. Learn to love, change the world." David Leija

tkomovement.com

This book belongs to

_____

tkomovement.com

This book is dedicated to the one person who taught me the values, principles, and lessons in life which this book and its series are based on.

To the world, you are known as Velma. To me, you are known as Mom.

tkomovement.com

Introduction....

This book is the first in a series by author David Leija, designed to help your child on lessons pertaining to diversity, shyness, tolerance, and other lessons that challenge our children in everyday life. We thank you for your purchase and hope you and your child enjoy reading TK's First Lesson

TK's First Lesson

TK and Toby looked alike;
twin brothers down to the
stripes.

The two brothers loved to play, running and jumping every day.

As they went to the pond for a drink, the reflection they saw made them think.

"Who is that, that I see? Why don't you look like me?"

They both ran home to talk to mom, wondering what was going on.

"Mommy! Mommy, come and see! Why doesn't TK look like me?"

Mother said, "What do you mean? You are brothers, don't be mean!"

13

"No, no, that can't be right! I am orange, and he is white."

"My little cubs, I will explain. You can be different and also be the same."

"You both love to run, jump and play. Does that make you different in any way?"

"Four legs, two eyes, and a tail, too. I see no differences as I look at you."

"The color of your coat is a small part. What really counts is in your heart."

"Being kind and respectful to all is not hard to do at all."

"Look at those flowers in the field below; all of those colors, bright like a rainbow."

"Would it be as pretty if all were the same? Imagine no color, only shades of grey."

29

"You both are colors in the field of life, made to stand out in the bright sunlight."

TK and Toby continued to play, remembering the lessons they were taught that day.

33

"We are all equal from within, and it's not the color of your skin that decides in life if you lose or win."

tkomovement.com

ANTI-BULLYING PLEDGE

✔ I will not bully anyone.

✔ I will be kind to everyone.

✔ I will speak out and report any bullying.

Name: _____   Date: _____

tkomovement.com

TKO (Tolerance Kindness Overcomes) is a brand and organization that strives to take concrete action steps to help prevent bullying. TKO provides anti-bullying education and partners with organizations that work to reduce the devastating effects of bullying. TKO is also committed to inclusion, equality, community outreach, and charitable giving. A portion of the proceeds generated from TKO merchandise purchases is dedicated to assuring that this good work continues.

Visit tkomovement.com to learn more about TKO and shop the entire TKO product line. We appreciate your support and hope you enjoyed TK's First Lesson.

Written by
David Leija

Illustrated by
Stevie Cortez

Contributors

Tim Tansil   **Ray Rodriguez**   **Johnny Casarez**

Made in the USA
Columbia, SC
13 March 2019